Hare and the Easter Eggs

Alison Uttley
pictures by Margaret Tempest

GALLERY BOOKS
An Imprint of W. H. Smith Publishers Inc.
112 Madison Avenue
New York City 10016

First published in the United States by Gallery Books,
an imprint of W.H. Smith Publishers Inc.,
112 Madison Avenue, New York, New York 10016.

First published 1952.
Text copyright © The Alison Uttley Literary Property Trust 1986.
Illustrations copyright © The Estate of Margaret Tempest 1986.
This arrangement © William Collins Sons & Co Ltd 1990
Produced for Gallery Books by Joshua Morris Publishing, Inc.
in association with William Collins Sons & Co Ltd.
All rights reserved.
Decorated capital by Mary Cooper.
Alison Uttley's original story has been abridged for this book.
ISBN 0-8317-5625-X
Printed in Great Britain

Gallery Books are available for bulk purchase for sales
promotions and premium use. For details write or telephone
the Manager of Special Sales, W.H. Smith Publishers, Inc.,
112 Madison Avenue, New York, New York 10016. (212) 532-6600

FOREWORD

Of course you must understand that Grey Rabbit's home had no electric light or gas. The candles were made from the pith of rushes dipped in wax from the wild bees' nests, which Squirrel found. Water there was in plenty, but it did not come from a faucet. It flowed from a spring outside, which rose up from the ground and went to a brook. Grey Rabbit cooked on a wood fire for there was no coal in that part of the country. Tea did not come from India, but from a little herb known very well to country people, who once dried it and used it in their cottage homes. Bread was baked from wheat ears, which Hare and Grey Rabbit gleaned in the cornfields.

The doormats were braided rushes, like country-made mats, and cushions were stuffed with wool gathered from the hedges where sheep had pushed through the thorns. As for the looking-glass, Grey Rabbit found the glass, dropped from a lady's handbag, and Mole made a frame for it. Usually the animals gazed at themselves in the still pools as so many country children have done. The country ways of Grey Rabbit were the country ways known to the author.

One evening in spring, Hare was dancing along the fields, skipping and tripping and bowing to the rabbits, when a sudden thought came into his head. Of course, as it was the month of March he was feeling exciting and wild, for all hares are mad in March and our friend Hare was no exception.

"I'll go to the village," said he to the world. "I'll go and see what there is to be seen and tell them at home all about it. I feel very brave tonight. I'm not scared of anything."

He stuck a primrose in his coat for luck and a buttercup in his collar for bravery, and he cut a slim hazel switch with buds dangling from it, just in case.

"Now I can face anybody," he said.

"I'll look at the village shop and see if Mrs. Bunting and the shop bell are still there."

It was dusk when he reached the village and the children were indoors having tea. Not even a dog or cat was to be seen. Hare leapt softly and swiftly down the cobbled street with a glance at the cottage where the old lace-maker lived and a peep at the blacksmith's and a wink at the white horse on the green.

He gave a chirrup of joy when he saw that the shop was still open. Brushes hung at the door and jars of sweets in the window shone with many colors in the dim light of the lamp.

Hare crept close. It was a lovely sight! Trains and tops, dolls and toy horses, cakes and cookies were there.

Then he opened his eyes very wide, for he saw something strange in the medley of toys and food. On a dish lay a pile of chocolate eggs with sugary flowers and "Happy Easter" written upon them. Ribbons were tied around them in blue, pink and yellow bows.

"Eggs! Enormous eggs! Eggs brown as earth. Beautiful eggs!" whispered Hare.

He stared and licked his lips.

"What kind of hen lays these pretty eggs? Ribbons on them! What would Grey Rabbit say? I should like to take her one, and Squirrel one and me one."

He pressed closer to the glass and his long ears flapped against the pane. Then footsteps came down the street, and he slipped into the shadows and crouched there dark as night.

A woman stopped at the shop window. She smiled when she saw the Easter eggs. She lifted the door latch and pushed open the door. A loud tinkle-tinkle came from the bell hanging above it.

"The bell's still there," thought Hare. "It's telling who comes into the shop."

"Good evening, Mrs. Bunting," called the woman.

"Good evening, Mrs. Snowball," replied Mrs. Bunting.

"Those are nice Easter eggs, Mrs. Bunting," said Mrs. Snowball. "How much are they?"

"Sixpence each," replied Mrs. Bunting, and she reached the dish from the window.

Hare crept into the shop and stood by Mrs. Snowball's skirts.

Mrs. Snowball chose her egg and while the two women chatted, Hare moved around. He stretched out a furry paw, he took a leap, and he snatched a chocolate egg. In a moment he was gone, out into the dusk.

"Oh! Oh!" cried Mrs. Bunting. "What was that?"

"I didn't see anything," said Mrs. Snowball. "Was it a cat?"

"I don't know what it was. Something took an egg," cried Mrs. Bunting. They both ran to the shop door, but Hare was already far away, running like the wind.

"You can't catch me," laughed Hare, as he leapt along the fields, squeezing the egg under his arm. Then he stopped to look at it. His warm fur had softened the chocolate and his fist went through. He pulled out a fluffy chicken made of silk and wool.

"Not real, but a good show," said Hare. He licked his paws and then licked the egg.

"Mmm! Delicious!" he cried, and soon the egg disappeared.

"That's the best egg I've ever tasted," he said, and he ran across the common and dashed into the little house where Grey Rabbit was cooking supper. A candle fluttered its yellow flame and the fire crackled comfortably on the hearth. Squirrel sat there making the toast.

"Here you come at last, Hare," cried Squirrel. "What have you been eating? You are brown and dirty."

"Not dirt, Squirrel. It's chocolate. I've eaten an egg laid by an Easter hen and it was made of chocolate," said Hare proudly.

"Chocolate egg?" cried Grey Rabbit. "Where was it?"

"In the village shop," said Hare. "I took it right under the nose of Mrs. Bunting."

"Hare! You stole it!" cried Grey Rabbit.

"I shall go and pay for it," explained Hare. "It was sixpence."

"You took an egg and you ate it all yourself," said Squirrel. "Greedy Hare!"

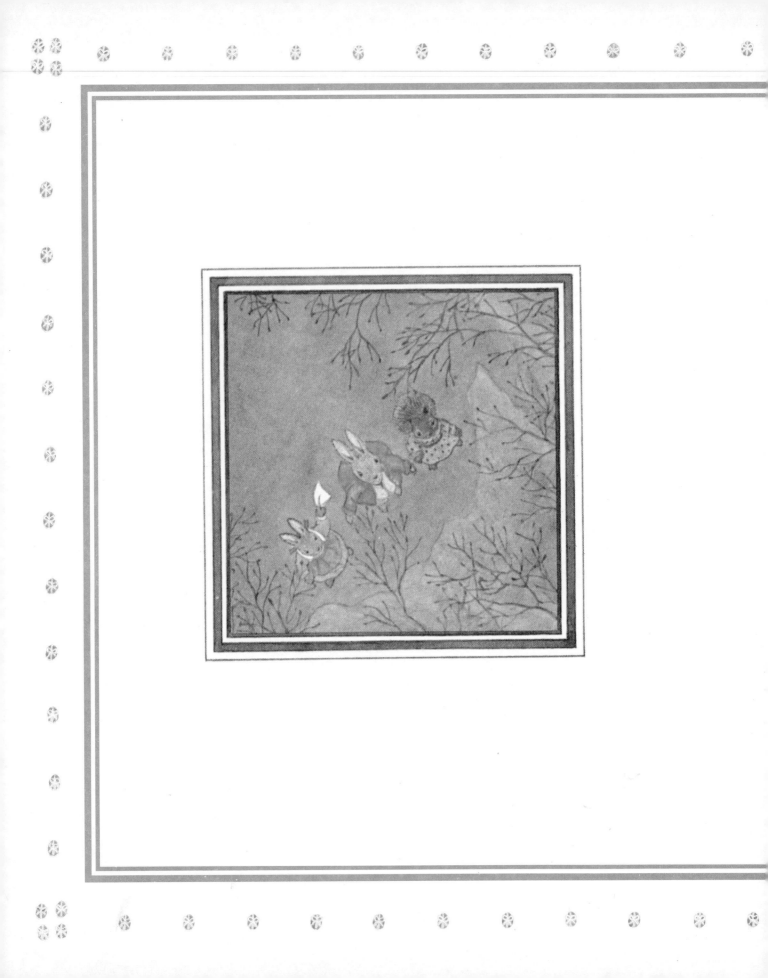

"I brought you the ribbon, Squirrel, and the little fluffy chicken inside the egg is for Grey Rabbit," said Hare, bringing the ribbon and the chicken from his pocket. Squirrel tied the ribbon around her waist and Grey Rabbit stroked the toy chicken.

"And did an Easter hen lay these?" they asked.

All evening they talked of Easter eggs, and the next morning Squirrel spoke to old Hedgehog when he came with the milk.

"Have you ever seen an Easter egg, Hedgehog?"

Hedgehog set down his pails.

"I don't know what it is," said he. "You'd better ask Wise Owl."

After breakfast the three locked the door and set off for Wise Owl's house. They rang the little silver bell and they stood in a row under the tree waiting for him.

"Who's there?" hooted Wise Owl very crossly. "Go away or I'll eat you."

"Please, Wise Owl…" began Grey Rabbit, waving her handkerchief for a truce.

"We want to know…" added Squirrel, stammering with fright.

"About Easter Eggs," shouted Hare in a loud voice.

"I've a good mind to tell you nothing," said Wise Owl, frowning at the noisy Hare.

"Yes, Wise Owl," said Grey Rabbit meekly.

"Easter Eggs come at Easter," said Wise Owl. "The church bells ring, and the little birds sing, and the sun dances on Easter morning."

He blinked and yawned and went to bed, banging his door so that the trunk shook.

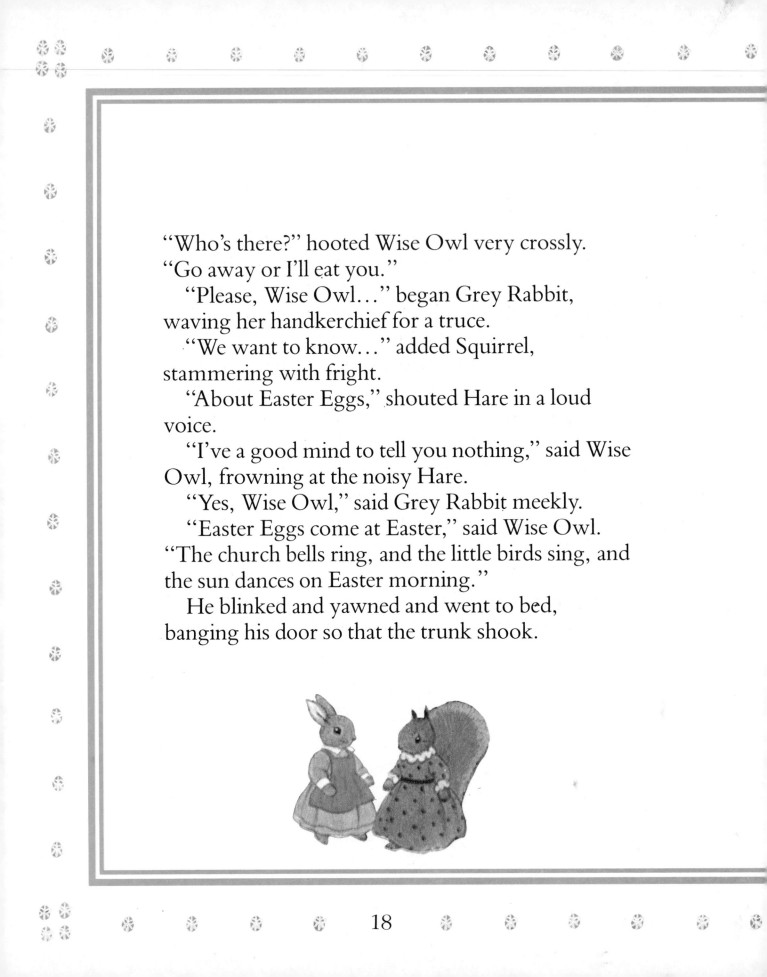

"He won't tell us any more," said Grey Rabbit. "Let us go away quickly before he eats us."

Grey Rabbit and Squirrel went home, but Hare leapt aside and ran across the fields. He tapped on Mole's door.

"Moldy Warp? Quick! Are you at home?" he called.

"What's the hurry, Hare?" asked the Mole, coming quietly around the corner with his spade.

"Oh, Mole, I didn't see you. Can you lend me a silver penny, or a gold penny or anything?" he said.

Moldy Warp went into the underground house and brought up a fistful of gold coins.

"You can have these if you'll do something for me," he said. "They are real gold. I dug them up in the Roman field one day when I went to see Badger."

"Oh, thank you, Moldy Warp. You are a real friend," cried Hare, stuffing the coins in his pocket.

"I have a fancy for some eggs," said Moldy Warp. "You know the Speckledy Hen better than I do."

"I'll bring you some at once," said Hare, gladly.

Speckledy Hen was in the meadow, scratching among the daisies when Hare came up.

"Please, Speckledy Hen, can I have some eggs for Moldy Warp?" asked Hare.

"Very well. As it's nearly Easter," said the hen, and she filled the basket from the store of eggs in the barn. "These have been laid by my friends, but my own newly laid egg is for Grey Rabbit."

Hare carried the eggs to Mole.

"I'm going to be very busy," said Moldy Warp. "Don't come here again, Hare. I'm getting ready for Easter."

He carried the eggs indoors and shut the door.

When Hare got to the little house he kept jingling the coins in his pocket.

"What makes the jingle-jangle, Hare? What is in your pocket?" asked Squirrel.

"It's a secret," said Hare. "A precious secret."

He took out his watch and shook it and changed the hands to make the time pass more quickly. "I'm going out again tonight," he announced.

As soon as tea was over he started. He took the way to the village, for he wanted another look at the Easter eggs, and he intended to pop a gold coin inside the shop door.

He had some difficulty in getting to the shop, for children were looking in the window, and he had to wait until they went away. When all was safe, he darted across the road.

"One for Hare and one for Squirrel and one for Grey Rabbit and one for Wise Owl and one for Hedgehog and one for Hare and one for Fuzzypeg," he murmured, counting the eggs. "How many is that? I can only count up to seven."

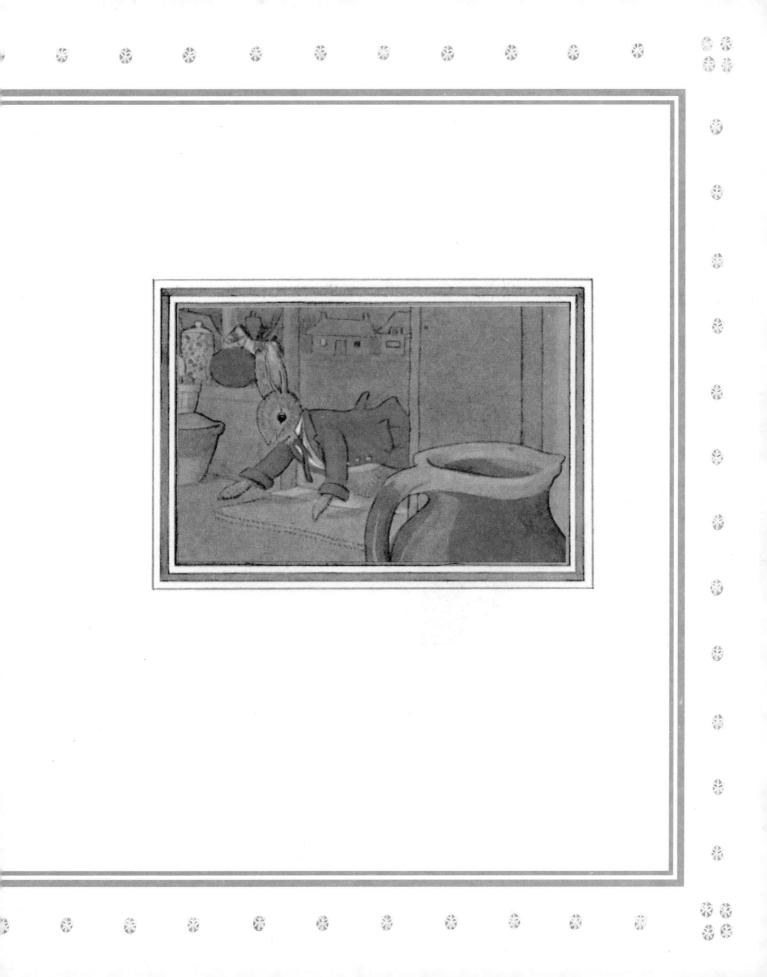

He leaned against the door, but it was not fastened, and Hare's fat little body fell inside the shop.

"Tinkle! Tinkle! Tinkle!" cried the little bell in its shrillest tone. "Tinkle! Mrs. Bunting! Tinkle!"

Mrs. Bunting heard the jingling bell, but she stopped to take the kettle off the fire in the back room. That gave Hare his chance. He dived into a brown jug which stood nearby. It was such a big jug that he was completely hidden, and he fell on his nose with his legs curled around him.

Mrs. Bunting looked over the counter suspiciously and then she went to the door.

She locked and bolted the door. She took the money from the till and turned down the lamp. Then she went to the back room and shut the door.

Hare slowly pushed up his long ears, his round head and his astonished eyes. There, watching him, sat a fine Tabby Cat. The two stared hard at each other.

"A Tabby," murmured Hare. "My whiskers! A Tabby."

"A jugged Hare, as sure as I'm alive," said the Tabby.

"Good evening," said Hare, and he scrambled out and made a deep bow with his paw on his heart.

"Gracious me!" exclaimed the Tabby. "It's Mister Hare as I've heard of."

"At your service, Ma'am," said Hare politely.

"Shhh!" cried the Cat, and Hare leapt back in the jug as the door opened and Mrs. Bunting appeared.

"What is it, Puss?" she asked. "Come along and have supper with me."

"Meow! Meow!" cried the Cat.

"Oh, very well! Perhaps there's a mouse," said Mrs. Bunting.

She fetched a saucerful of milk and shut the door.

"You can come out now," whispered the Cat. "She'll go to bed soon."

Hare climbed out clutching the gold coins.

"I've come to buy some Easter eggs," said he. "Here's the money."

"This will buy up the shop," said the Cat. "We never see any gold, only sixpence and pennies."

Mrs. Bunting's footsteps thudded up the stairs into the bedroom over the shop.

"Now we can talk," said the Cat with relief. "I want to hear about you and Squirrel and Grey Rabbit. I'll get you a bite to eat first."

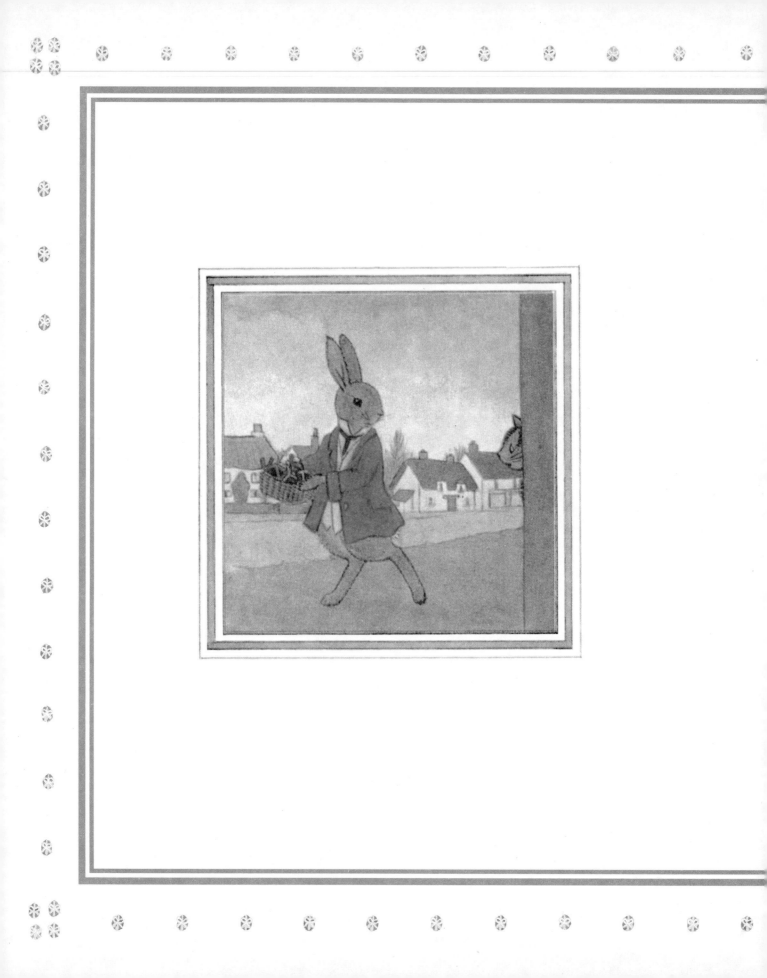

She fetched some sausages and ham from the counter and sugary buns from the window.

"Eat these, Hare," she said, and Hare gobbled them up. He told all his adventures and many more, and the Cat thought he was the bravest, boldest animal she had ever met.

Then his head nodded, and he slept.

Dawn came with the crowing of cocks and the clamor of the alarm clock, and Hare opened his eyes.

"It's time you were off, Hare. Mrs. Bunting gets up when the alarm sounds," said the Cat. "I'll open the door for you."

Hare packed the Easter eggs in a basket while the Cat deftly drew the bolts and unlocked the door. The little bell was all ready to cry "Tinkle! Tinkle!" but the Cat was prepared.

"No, you don't," said she, and she wrapped a cloth round the clapping tongue. "Now you can't speak."

Puss opened the door and the sweet morning air came pouring in. The bell shook and leapt on its spring, but no sound ever came. Hare poured his gold coins on the dish, and seized the basket of eggs.

"Good-bye, Mistress Tabby," he said. "Thank you very much for your kindness."

"Puss! Puss!" called a voice, and Hare saw Mrs. Bunting in her dressing gown. "Puss! Have you opened the door? Puss, where are the Easter eggs? Puss, who put that money there?"

Hare didn't wait any longer.

Grey Rabbit and Squirrel were fast asleep, but they had left the door unlocked for Hare to enter. Hare hid the chocolate eggs in the empty beehive in the garden, and then he crept into bed.

"Would you like an Easter party?" asked Grey Rabbit after breakfast. "We will invite our friends to see the sun dance on Easter morning."

"Oh yes," cried Squirrel.

"I'll make some Easter cakes and you shall send the invitations," said Grey Rabbit, getting down the yellow bowl.

She made a heap of tiny cakes, each in the shape of a moon, with caraway seeds on the top. Squirrel and Hare scribbled the invitations on primrose petals. Squirrel was a poor writer and Hare couldn't spell, so they put on the letter E and nothing else. Robin had to explain E was an Easter party as he delivered the letters.

Squirrel had knitted an egg for Grey Rabbit. She made it of blue wool and she stuffed it with nuts.

Rat had carved a little bone egg which opened. Inside he put a wooden thimble for Grey Rabbit and a few thorn pins.

On Easter morning Grey Rabbit, Squirrel and Hare went to the garden in the early light, but already the birds were singing their Easter hymn. Hare was very excited about something. Grey Rabbit wondered why he kept looking at the beehive.

"We haven't any bees, Hare," she reminded him.

Away in the east the sky was bathed in golden light, and rosy clouds floated above the rising sun.

Then Moldy Warp brought his basket of colored eggs.

"These are magical eggs," said Grey Rabbit. "How ever did you make them, Moldy Warp?"

Rat came forward with his bone egg and Grey Rabbit opened it and found the thimble and pins.

"How clever of you to carve this little Easter egg!" said Grey Rabbit.

Squirrel offered her funny knitted egg, crooked and fat, and Grey Rabbit hugged her friend.

Next, old Hedgehog and Fuzzypeg came with duck eggs, and the Speckledy Hen brought her own newly laid egg.

All this time Hare had been dodging backward and forward, glancing at the beehive, and then going away. At last he lifted the straw skep and brought out the chocolate eggs.

"Grey Rabbit, Squirrel, Hedgehog family, Speckledy Hen, Moldy Warp, and all, I wish you a Happy Easter," he said. On the grass he spread the chocolate eggs with their bright ribbons and curly lettering, and everybody cried out in surprise and pleasure.

"Chocolate eggs! Chocolate eggs! Easter eggs! Easter eggs for children and rabbits."

"But not for hares," hooted Wise Owl, flying over. He dived down and seized an egg. He pierced it with his beak and brought out the fluffy toy chick.

"Bah! Not real! A trick!" he snorted, and away he flew.

Hare mopped his forehead. Squirrel came from the shelter of her spreading tail.

Grey Rabbit took the apron from her face.

"Where did these come from?" she asked faintly.

"I bought them," said Hare. "I paid for them, and Moldy Warp gave me the money. They are from Moldy Warp and me."

Moldy Warp looked surprised, and he stroked one of the eggs.

They sat on the ground in a circle and drank tiny glasses of primrose wine and ate bits of the Easter eggs.

"Happy Easter," they said to one another, holding their glasses high.

"We should like to hear how Mister Hare was able to get these wonderful eggs," said Old Hedgehog.

So Hare told his adventure, and they all thought he was a very clever hare.

"Of course I am," said Hare. "I always knew it. I've been telling you for years, but you wouldn't believe me."